P9-CBM-618

Make and Eat

Bread & Pizzas

Susannah Blake

PowerKiDS press

New York

Published in 2009 by The Rosen Publishing Group Inc.
29 East 21st Street, New York, NY 10010

First Edition

Senior editor: Jennifer Schofield
Designer: Jane Hawkins
Photographer: Andy Crawford
Proofreader: Susie Brooks

Library of Congress Cataloging-in-Publication Data

Blake, Susannah.
Bread and pizzas / Susannah Blake. — 1st ed.
p. cm. — (Make and eat)
Includes index.
ISBN 978-1-4358-2858-2 (lib. binding)
ISBN 978-1-4358-2932-9 (paperback)
ISBN 978-1-4358-2936-7 (6-pack)
1. Bread—Juvenile literature. 2. Pizza—Juvenile literature. I. Title.
TX769.B5877 2009
641.8'15—dc22
2008025796

Manufactured in China

Acknowledgements:
The author and publisher would like to thank the following models: Adam Menditta, Jade Campbell, Aneesa Qureshi, Taylor Fulton, Emel Auguspan, Kaine Zachary Levy, Ammar Duffus, Claire Shanahan.

Web Sites

Due to the changing nature of Internet links, PowerKids Press has developed an online list of Web sites related to the subject of this book. This site is updated regularly. Please use this link to access this list: www.powerkidslinks.com/mae/brpizzas

Note to parents and teachers:
The recipes in this book are intended to be made by children. However, we recommend adult supervision at all times, especially when using kitchen equipment, since the Publisher cannot be held responsible for any injury.

Contents

All about bread and pizza	4
Soda bread	6
Cornbread	8
Whole-wheat bread	10
Cottage bread	12
Garlic focaccia	14
Fruity buns	16
Pizza	18
Tasty calzone	20
Glossary and Extra Information	22
Equipment	23
Index	24

All about bread and pizza

People have eaten bread for thousands of years. Loaves have been found in ancient Egyptian tombs that are over 5,000 years old. Today, there are many kinds of bread from all over the world, and the same dough that is used to make bread can also be used to make pizza.

MAKING DOUGH

Bread dough is usually made from four ingredients—flour, a leavening ingredient, such as yeast, to make it rise, salt, and a liquid, such as water. The flour used to make dough usually comes from ground wheat, but flour from other grains, such as rye and corn, can also be used.

KNEADING DOUGH

Before baking it to make bread, dough must be kneaded. To knead dough, sprinkle some flour on your work surface, then turn the dough out onto the surface. Using the heel of your hands, press down on the dough to flatten it. Fold the dough over into a ball shape and press it again with the heel of your hand. Continue pressing and folding, trying to end up with the dough in a ball-shape each time. This basic dough can be made into rounds to make pizzas or shaped into loaves or rolls. Extra ingredients, such as dried fruit and herbs, can be added to give the bread a unique flavor.

BREAD FROM AROUND THE WORLD

There are hundreds of different types of bread from around the world. They are made from different combinations of the basic ingredients and are baked in different ways to produce their unique shape, taste, and texture. Classic breads include Indian naan, which is a flattish, oval-shaped bread cooked on a griddle. The Jewish bagel is a ring-shaped roll—the dough is shaped, then boiled or steamed before baking to give it a chewy texture. The French stick is a white, crusty loaf that can be large or small. Caribbean buns are a dense, spicy teabread flavored with molasses and studded with dried fruit.

GET STARTED!

In this book, you can learn to make all kinds of bread and pizza. All the recipes use everyday kitchen equipment, such as knives, spoons, forks, and cutting boards. You can see pictures of the different equipment that you may need on page 23. Before you start, check that you have all the equipment that you will need and make a list of any ingredients that you need to buy. Make sure that there is an adult to help you, especially with the recipes that involve using the stove or oven.

When you have everything you need, make sure all the kitchen surfaces are clean, and wash your hands well with soap and water. If you have long hair, tie it back. Always wash raw fruits and vegetables under cold running water before preparing or cooking them. This will help to remove any dirt and germs. Then, put on an apron and get cooking!

Soda bread

Breads leavened using yeast need to be left to rise. This traditional Irish bread uses baking soda and cream of tartar instead of yeast, so it can be put straight in the oven.

INGREDIENTS

For 1 loaf:

- 3 tbsp butter, plus extra for greasing
- 1¾ cups whole-wheat flour, plus extra for dusting
- 1¾ cups all-purpose flour
- 1 tsp salt
- 2 tsp baking soda
- 2 tsp cream of tartar
- 1 tsp sugar
- ¾ cup milk
- ¾ cup plain yogurt

EXTRA EQUIPMENT

- baking sheet
- wire rack
- sieve

Ask an adult to help you use the oven.

1 Preheat the oven to 375°F (190°C). Rub a little butter on the baking sheet to coat it all over.

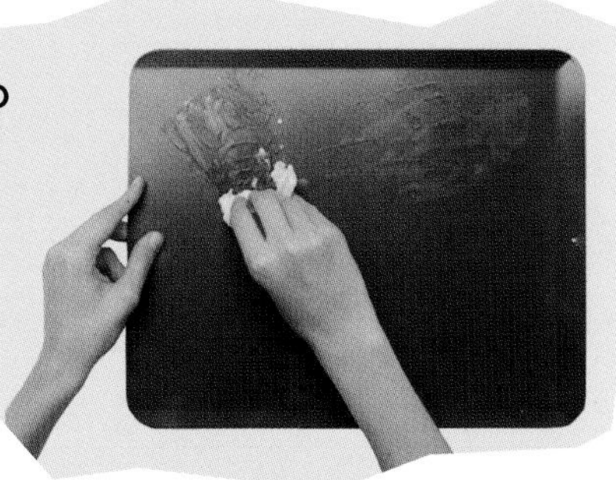

2 Hold the sieve over a bowl and pour the whole-wheat and white flours, salt, baking soda, and cream of tartar into it. Tap the side of the sieve until the ingredients have fallen into the bowl below.

3 Cut the butter into small pieces, then add them to the flour mixture.

4 Rub the butter into the flour until the mixture looks like breadcrumbs. Stir in the sugar.

5 Make a well in the middle of the flour crumbs. Mix the milk and yogurt together, and pour the mixture into the well. Stir to make a soft dough. If the dough is dry, add a little more milk. If the mixture is too wet, add a sprinkle more flour.

6 Sprinkle a little flour on your work surface. Turn the dough onto the work surface and shape it into a round.

7 Place the round on a baking sheet and, with a sharp knife, mark a cross in the top of the loaf. Cut quite deep into the dough, but not all the way through.

8 Sprinkle a little more flour over the top of the loaf and put it in the oven. Bake it for about 40 minutes until well risen.

9 When the loaf is baked, put it on a wire rack to cool. Serve it warm with butter.

IS IT BAKED?

To check if bread is baked, use oven gloves to take the loaf out of the oven. Holding the loaf in a gloved hand, remove the other glove and tap the base of the loaf. It should sound hollow if it is baked through. If it is not baked, put the loaf in the oven for a few more minutes then check it again.

Cornbread

This bread is made using cornmeal. The cornmeal gives the bread a lovely yellow color and a distinctive taste. Baking powder makes this bread rise.

INGREDIENTS

For 1 loaf:

- 4 tbsp sunflower oil, plus extra for greasing
- 1¼ cups cornmeal
- 1 cup all-purpose flour
- 1 tbsp sugar • ¼ tsp salt
- 1 tbsp baking powder • 2 eggs
- ⅔ cup milk • ½ cup plain yogurt

EXTRA EQUIPMENT

- 8 in. (20cm) square cake pan
- metal skewer

Ask an adult to help you use the oven.

1 Preheat the oven to 400°F (200°C). Rub a little oil inside the cake pan, making sure the surfaces are coated all over.

2 Put the cornmeal, flour, sugar, salt, and baking powder in a bowl. Mix them together and make a well in the middle. Set aside for later.

3 Break the eggs into another bowl and beat them with a fork. Add the yogurt, milk, and sunflower oil, and stir.

4 Pour the egg mix into the well in the cornmeal. Stir the ingredients together, bringing the dry ingredients into the middle of the bowl.

AMAZING MAIZE

Cornmeal is made from corn or maize, which is a major crop in the United States. Bread made from cornmeal is very popular and is served as an accompaniment to dishes such as fried chicken. It is also used as the base for turkey stuffing.

5 Pour the batter into the pan. Make sure it goes into the corners of the pan. Bake the bread for about 25 minutes until it is firm and golden.

6 To check if the bread is baked, press a skewer into the middle, then gently pull it out. If it comes out clean, the cornbread is baked. If there are still crumbs on the skewer, put the bread back in the oven for a few more minutes.

7 When the bread is baked, remove the pan from the oven and put it on a heatproof surface. Leave the bread to cool in the pan for about 10 minutes.

8 Wearing an oven mitt, run a knife around the inside edges of the pan to loosen the bread. Hold a board on top of the pan and flip over the board and pan. If you lift the pan, the bread should come out. Cut the bread into wedges and serve them warm.

Whole-wheat bread

This recipe is based on the recipe for traditional Grant loaves. It is popular because the dough does not need to be kneaded before it is put into pans.

INGREDIENTS

For 2 loaves:

- oil, for greasing
- 6½ cups whole-wheat bread flour
- 2 tsp salt • 3⅓ cups warm water
- 2¼ tsp active dry yeast
- 2 tsp dark brown sugar

EXTRA EQUIPMENT

- 2 x 2 lb. loaf pans • sieve
- plastic wrap • wire rack

Ask an adult to help you use the oven.

1 Rub a little oil inside each loaf pan, making sure the surface is thoroughly coated. Put the pans in a warm place.

2 Mix the flour and salt together and sieve them into a bowl. Make a well in the center of the dry ingredients. Put the bowl in a warm place.

3 Pour ⅔ cup of warm water into a measuring jug. Check the temperature by putting your finger in the water. It should feel warm to the touch, but not hot. Sprinkle in the yeast and leave it to stand for 1 minute. Then sprinkle in the sugar, stir, and leave to stand for 10 minutes.

YEAST

Yeast is a type of fungus that grows quickly. As it grows, it produces bubbles of carbon dioxide, which make the bread rise. The perfect temperature for yeast to grow in is 100°F (38°C). Since it is killed in temperatures over 140°F (60°C), it is important to check that the water is not too hot before mixing it with the yeast.

4 Pour the yeast mix into the flour. Measure another 2¾ cups of warm water. Check the temperature, then pour it into the flour. Stir until the dough is well mixed.

5 Divide the dough between the two pans, flattening it slightly with the back of a spoon.

6 Tear off two pieces of plastic wrap and rub a little oil on each one. Cover each pan and put it in a warm place to rise for about 30 minutes, or until the dough has risen by one-third.

7 While the bread rises, preheat the oven to 400°F (200°C). When the loaves have risen, bake them for about 40 minutes.

8 Following the panel instructions on page 7, check if the bread is baked. When they are baked, turn the loaves out onto a wire rack and allow them to cool.

Cottage bread

This traditional English loaf has a distinctive shape. It can be made using white or whole-wheat flour and is delicious served warm with Cheddar cheese.

INGREDIENTS

For 1 loaf:

- 4¼ cups strong white bread flour, plus extra for dusting
- 1¾ tsp active dry yeast
- 1 tsp salt • 1½ cups warm water
- 1 tbsp sunflower oil, plus extra for oiling

EXTRA EQUIPMENT

- pastry brush • plastic wrap
- baking sheet • kitchen scissors
- wire rack

Ask an adult to help you use the oven.

1 Put the flour, yeast, and salt in a large bowl and mix them together. Make a well in the middle of the mixture.

2 Check the temperature of the water—it should feel warm, but not hot. Pour the water into the well in the flour and add the oil. Mix to make a rough dough.

3 Sprinkle a little flour on your work surface, then knead the dough for about 10 minutes until it is smooth and elastic. If the dough is sticky, sprinkle in a little more flour as you knead.

4 Brush a little sunflower oil inside a clean bowl. Put the dough in the bowl, then brush the top with a little oil. Cover the bowl with plastic wrap and leave it to stand in a warm place for 45 minutes, or until it has doubled in size.

5 When it has risen, punch the dough a couple of times to get rid of the air.

6 Sprinkle your work surface with a little flour and knead the dough for about 2 minutes. Cut off about one-third of the dough and shape both pieces into round balls.

7 Grease a baking sheet then dust it with flour. Put the larger ball on the sheet and brush it with water. Place the second ball on top. Dip two fingers in flour, then press them down into the middle of the two balls to stick them together. Using kitchen scissors, make little snips around the edge of the top ball.

8 Grease some plastic wrap with oil, then use it to cover the dough. Leave the dough to rise in a warm place for 40 minutes.

9 About 15 minutes before the end of rising time, preheat the oven to 375°F (190°C). Remove the plastic wrap and sprinkle the bread with a light dusting of flour.

10 Bake the bread for about 40 minutes until golden brown, then use oven gloves to place it on a wire rack to cool before serving.

SHAPING LOAVES

Bread dough can be shaped into all kinds of loaves before baking: rings, rounds, and sticks. Many shapes are specific to countries. In France, the traditional shaped loaf is a baton, or stick. In Italy, there is the flat, dimpled focaccia (see page 14) and the flat, oval, or rectangular ciabatta. In regions of Spain and Portugal, you will find crusty round loaves.

Garlic focaccia

This is a classic Italian bread. It can be plain or flavored with herbs, onions, or other ingredients, such as sun-dried tomatoes.

INGREDIENTS

For two loaves:

- 3¾ cups strong white bread flour, plus extra for dusting
- 2¼ tsp active dry yeast
- 1 tsp salt • 1⅓ cups warm water
- 6 tsp olive oil
- sea salt • 3 garlic cloves, chopped

EXTRA EQUIPMENT

- sieve • plastic wrap • rolling pin
- 2 x 10 in. (25cm) pizza or cake pans
- wire rack

Ask an adult to help you use the oven.

1 Mix the flour, yeast, and salt together, then sieve them into a bowl. Make a well in the middle of the mixture.

2 Check the temperature of the water by putting your finger into it. It should feel just warm, but not hot.

3 Pour the water into the well in the flour and add 3 tsp of olive oil. Stir together to make a soft dough.

THE HOME OF FOCACCIA

Focaccia is particularly associated with Liguria in Italy. This region stretches along the coast in the northwest of the country. Another famous specialty of the region is *pesto*—a pasta sauce made of basil, pine nuts, garlic, and cheese.

4 Sprinkle a little flour on your work surface, then knead the dough for about 10 minutes. If the dough is sticky, continue sprinkling in a little more flour as you work.

5 Wash your hands, then rub a little oil inside a clean bowl. Put the dough inside and pat your oily hands on the dough to make it oily, too. Cover the bowl with plastic wrap and leave it to rise in a warm place for 1 hour.

6 When the dough has risen, sprinkle your work surface with a little flour and transfer the dough to it. Press down on the dough to expel some of the air. Divide the dough into two equal pieces, then roll it into two balls. Roll each piece into 10-in. (25-cm) rounds and place inside cake or pizza pans.

7 Cover the pans with plastic wrap and leave to rise in a warm place for about 30 minutes. Meanwhile, preheat the oven to 400°F (200°C).

8 Uncover the pans and poke the dough with your fingertips to make dimples all over the surface. Drizzle the rest of the olive oil over the top, and sprinkle a little sea salt on each one. Sprinkle the chopped garlic on top.

9 Bake for 25–30 minutes until the loaves are golden. When they are baked, use a spatula to lift the loaves from the pans and transfer them to a wire rack. Serve warm.

Fruity buns

These sweet buns are studded with plump raisins. They are delicious when eaten warm.

INGREDIENTS

For 12:

- 3 tbsp butter
- 3¾ cups strong white bread flour, plus extra for dusting
- 2¼ tsp active dry yeast
- 1 tsp salt • 3 tbsp sugar
- 1 tsp ground cinnamon
- 1 cup raisins • 1⅛ cups warm water
- sunflower oil • milk, for brushing

EXTRA EQUIPMENT

- sieve • plastic wrap • baking sheet
- pastry brush • wire rack

Ask an adult to help you use the oven.

1 Melt the butter over low heat then set it aside.

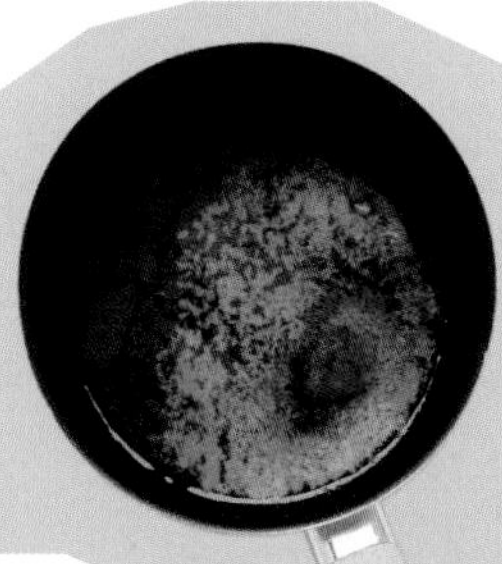

2 Combine the flour, yeast, salt, sugar, and cinnamon, and sieve them into a clean bowl.

3 Stir the raisins into the flour mix. Make a well in the middle.

4 Check the temperature of the water. It should feel warm, but not hot. Pour the water and cooled melted butter into the dry ingredients.

5 Fold in the ingredients to make a soft dough. If the dough is a little dry, add a drizzle more water. If it is a little sticky, add a sprinkle more flour.

6 Sprinkle flour on your work surface before kneading the dough for about 10 minutes. It should be smooth and elastic.

7 Brush a little oil inside a bowl and put the dough in it. Then brush the top of the dough with a little oil.

8 Cover the bowl with plastic wrap and leave it in a warm place for 45 minutes. In the meantime, rub a baking sheet with a little oil to grease it.

9 Sprinkle your work surface with flour and knead the dough for a minute. Divide the dough into 12 pieces, and roll each piece into a ball.

10 Put the balls on the baking sheet and cover them with a kitchen towel. Leave them in a warm place for 30 minutes. Preheat the oven to 400°F (200°C).

11 Brush the buns with milk, then bake them for 20 minutes, or until risen and golden.

12 Take the buns out of the oven. Transfer them to a wire rack to cool before serving.

HOT CROSS BUNS

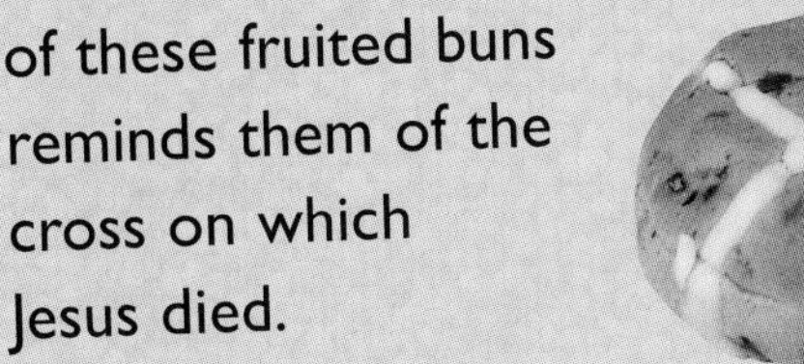

On Good Friday—the Friday before Easter Sunday—some Christians eat hot cross buns. The cross on top of these fruited buns reminds them of the cross on which Jesus died.

Pizza

This classic cheese and tomato pizza is called a Margarita. Once you have mastered this recipe, you can add different toppings, such as spicy sausage, olives, peppers, and tuna.

INGREDIENTS

For 4 pizzas:
- 1½ cups strong white bread flour
- 1 tsp active dry yeast
- ½ tsp salt
- ½ cup warm water
- 1 tbsp olive oil
- 6 tbsp fresh tomato sauce
- 3½ oz. (100g) grated mozzarella
- ground black pepper

EXTRA EQUIPMENT

- sieve
- plastic wrap
- rolling pin
- 2 baking sheets

Ask an adult to help you use the oven.

1 Sieve together the flour, yeast, and salt. Make a well in the middle of the mix.

2 Check the temperature of the water by putting your finger into it. It should feel just warm, but not hot.

3 Pour the water into the well and add the oil. Stir together to make a soft dough.

4 Sprinkle a little flour on your work surface, then put the dough on top. Sprinkle a little more flour on top of the dough, then knead it for about 10 minutes, until it is smooth and elastic. If the dough is sticky, continue sprinkling a little more flour on it as you work.

5 Wash your hands, then rub a little oil inside a clean bowl. Put the dough inside and pat your oily hands on the dough to make that oily, too. Cover the bowl with plastic wrap, and put it in a warm place for 1 hour until it has doubled in size.

6 About 15 minutes before the end of rising time, preheat the oven to 425°F (220°C).

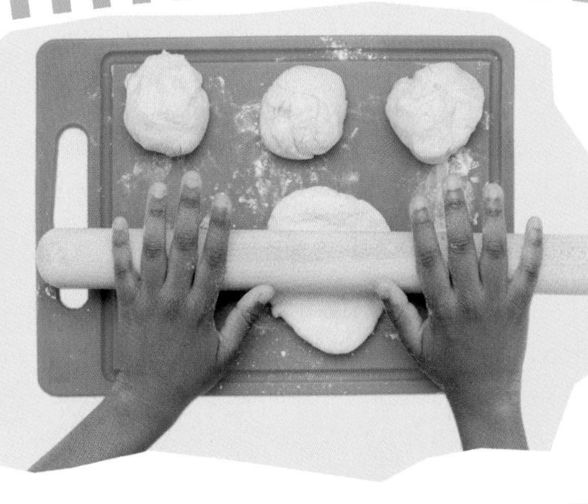

7 Sprinkle a little flour on the work surface and transfer the dough to it. Press down on the dough to get rid of some of the air. Cut the dough into four equal pieces. Using a rolling pin, roll each piece into a 5-in. (13-cm) round.

8 Arrange the rounds on baking sheets. Spread about 1 1/2 tbsp of tomato sauce on top of each one.

PIZZA OVENS

Traditionally, pizzas were baked in wood-fired brick ovens. The ovens were heated until they were very hot, and the pizzas were put into the oven and taken out on a long wooden paddle. You can still see this in some pizza restaurants today.

9 Sprinkle cheese on top of each pizza. Put the baking sheets in the oven, and bake for 12 minutes, until the pizzas are golden and crisp on the edges.

10 Wearing oven gloves, take the baking sheets from the oven and place them on a heatproof surface. When the pizza is cool enough, cut it into slices and serve.

Tasty calzone

When you cut into this calzone, you will find a pizza filling inside the crispy crust. You can use all kinds of pizza fillings inside a calzone—this one has ham, ricotta, and tomatoes.

INGREDIENTS

For 4 calzone:

- 3 cups strong white bread flour, plus extra for dusting
- $2\frac{1}{4}$ tsp active dry yeast
- 1 tsp salt
- 1 cup warm water
- 2 tbsp olive oil
- 3 ripe tomatoes
- $3\frac{1}{2}$ oz. (100g) ricotta
- 4 tbsp freshly grated Parmesan
- 3 oz. (85g) sliced ham
- 8 basil leaves
- black pepper

EXTRA EQUIPMENT

- sieve
- plastic wrap
- pastry brush
- rolling pin
- baking sheet

Ask an adult to help you use the oven.

1 Sieve together the flour, yeast, and salt. Make a well in the middle of the flour mix.

2 Check the temperature of the water. It should feel just warm, but not hot.

3 Pour the water into the well and add the oil. Stir together to make a soft dough.

4 Sprinkle flour on your work surface, then knead the dough for about 10 minutes until it is smooth and elastic. If the dough is sticky, continue sprinkling in a little more flour as you knead.

5 Brush a little oil inside a clean bowl. Put the dough inside and brush a little oil on top of the dough. Cover with plastic wrap and leave it to stand for 1 hour, until the dough has doubled in size. After 45 minutes, preheat the oven to 425°F (220°C).

6 In the meantime, make the filling. Slice the tomatoes in half. Press your thumb into the seeds to remove them, then cut out the woody stem and throw it away. Roughly chop the flesh and put it in a bowl.

7 Add the ricotta and Parmesan to the tomatoes. Tear the ham into pieces and add them to the bowl. Tear the basil leaves into pieces and add them to the bowl, too. Add freshly ground black pepper and stir.

8 Sprinkle flour on your work surface before pressing down on the dough to get rid of some of the air. Cut the dough into four pieces. Roll each piece into a 8-in. (20-cm) round.

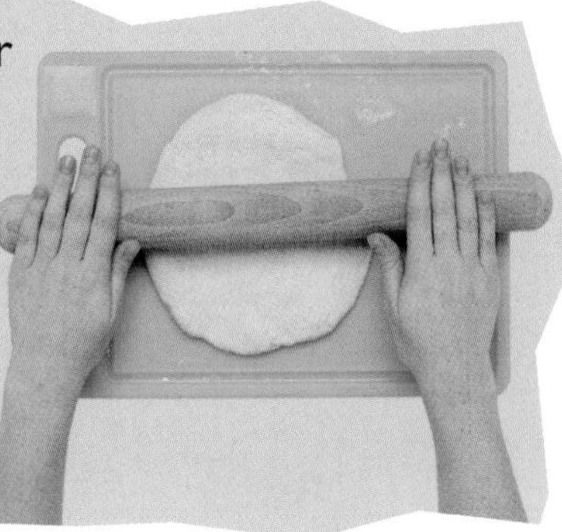

9 Spoon a quarter of the filling on half of each round, leaving a big border around the edge.

10 Fold over the top of the dough to make a half-moon shape. Press down around the outside, and twist the edge of the dough to seal it. Put the calzone on a baking sheet, brush with oil, and bake for 15 minutes until golden.

11 Wearing oven gloves, remove the baking sheet from the oven and put it on a heatproof surface. Transfer each calzone to a serving plate and serve.

Glossary

accompaniment Something that is served with a main meal.

carbon dioxide A colorless gas. Carbon dioxide reacts with leavening ingredients to form bubbles that make dough rise.

fungus A plant that has no leaves or flowers, which grows on other plants. Mushrooms, toadstools, and yeast are all kinds of fungus.

Grant loaves Traditional whole-wheat loaves made by a lady named Doris Grant in the 1940s.

griddle A metal plate that is heated and cooked on. Drop biscuits and flatbreads are made on griddles.

hollow When something is hollow it sounds empty, like there is space inside it.

knead To pull and stretch dough so that it becomes soft and elastic.

leavening ingredient The ingredient in baking that makes doughs and batters rise. Yeast, baking soda, and baking powder are all leavening ingredients.

molasses A sugary syrup used in baking.

rub in To work butter into flour using your hands, so that the resulting mix resembles fine breadcrumbs.

specialty Something for which an area or person is famous. For example, France's specialty bread is the baguette or French stick, and Italy's is the ciabatta or focaccia.

traditional When something is passed down from one generation to the next or is what is usually done.

wood-fired Heated by burning wood. Traditional pizza ovens are wood-fired.

BOOKS TO READ

Bread, Bread, Bread
by Ann Morris (Topeka Bindery, 1999)

Kitchen for Kids
by Jennifer Low (Whitecap Books, 2004)

MEASUREMENT CONVERSIONS

Liquid
1 cup = 8 fl. oz. (250 ml)

Flour
1 cup = 4 oz. (115g)
1 tbsp = 1/2 oz. (15g)

Butter
1 stick = 4 oz. (115g)
1 tbsp = 1/2 oz. (15g)

Sugar
1 cup = 9 oz. (225g)
1 tbsp = 1 oz. (28g)

EXTRA INFORMATION

These abbreviations have been used:

- tbsp—tablespoon • tsp—teaspoon
- oz.—ounce • lb.—pound
- ml—milliliter • g—gram • l—liter

To work out where the stove dial needs to be for high, medium, and low heat, count the marks on the dial and divide it by three. The top few are high and the bottom few are low. The in-between ones are medium.

All eggs are medium unless stated.

Equipment

ROLLING PIN
Round wooden rolling pins can be used to roll out bread and pizza dough.

WIRE RACK
Breads and cakes should always be cooled on a rack to allow air to circulate underneath.

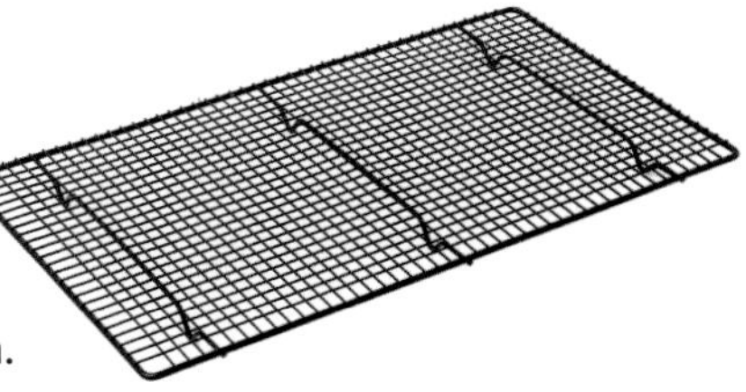

WOODEN SPOONS
Use these spoons to stir food when cooking or to mix batters and dough when making bread.

MEASURING JUG
Use this to measure liquids.

CUTTING BOARDS
Make sure you keep your cutting boards clean. Always use a different one for meat and vegetables.

PASTRY BRUSH
Use this to brush oils and milk on dough before it is baked.

BAKING PANS
These come in all shapes and sizes, so you can bake different-shaped loaves and cakes.

FOOD SCALE
Use a scale to measure dry and solid ingredients accurately.

METAL SKEWER
Skewers are useful for tespang whether bread is baked.

GRATER
Use to grate foods such as cheese and carrots. Keep your fingers away from the sharp teeth of the grater.

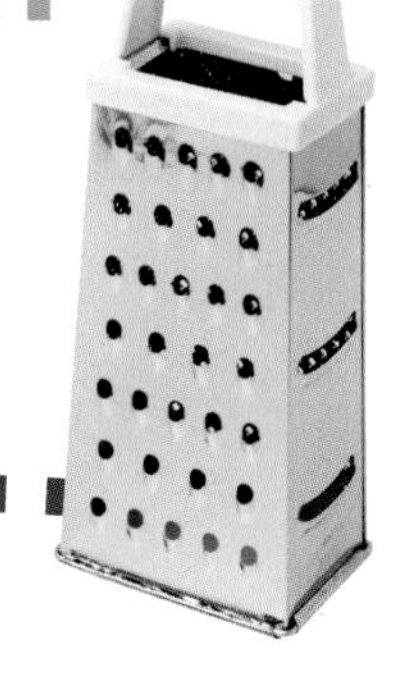

Index

bagels 5
baking powder 8, 22
baking soda 6, 22
black pepper 18, 20
butter 6, 16, 22

calzone 20-21
carbon dioxide 11, 22
Caribbean buns 5
Cheddar cheese 12
chicken 8, 22
ciabatta 13, 22
cinnamon 16
corn 4
cornbread 8–9
cornmeal 8
cottage bread 12–13
cream of tartar 6

dark brown sugar 10
dough 4, 13, 22
dried fruit 4, 5

Easter Sunday 17
eggs 8, 22
Egypt 4
England 12

flour 4, 22
  white 6, 8, 12, 14, 16, 18, 20
  whole-wheat 6, 10, 12
focaccia 13, 14–15, 22
French stick 5, 13, 22
fruity buns 16–17
fungus 11, 22

garlic 14
garlic focaccia 14–15
Good Friday 17
Grant loaves 10, 22
griddles 5, 22

ham 20
herbs 4, 14
  basil 14, 20
hot cross buns 17

India 5
Ireland 6
Italy 13, 14, 22

kneading 4, 10, 22

leavening 4, 6, 22

milk 4, 6, 8, 16
mozzarella cheese 18
mushrooms 22

naan 4

oil 8, 10, 12, 14, 16, 18, 20
olives 18
onions 14

Parmesan 20
peppers 18
pesto 14
pine nuts 14
pizza 4, 5, 18–19
  fillings 18, 20
  ovens 19, 22
Portugal 13

raisins 18
ricotta 20
rye 4

salt 4, 6, 8, 10, 14, 16, 18, 20
sausage 18
shaping bread 13
soda bread 6–7
Spain 13
sugar 6, 8, 16
sundried tomatoes 14

toadstools 22
tomatoes 20
  sauce 18
tuna 18
turkey 8

United States 8

water 4, 10, 11, 12, 14, 16, 18, 20
wheat 4
whole-wheat bread 10–11

yeast 4, 6, 10, 11, 12, 14, 16, 18, 20, 22
yogurt 6, 8